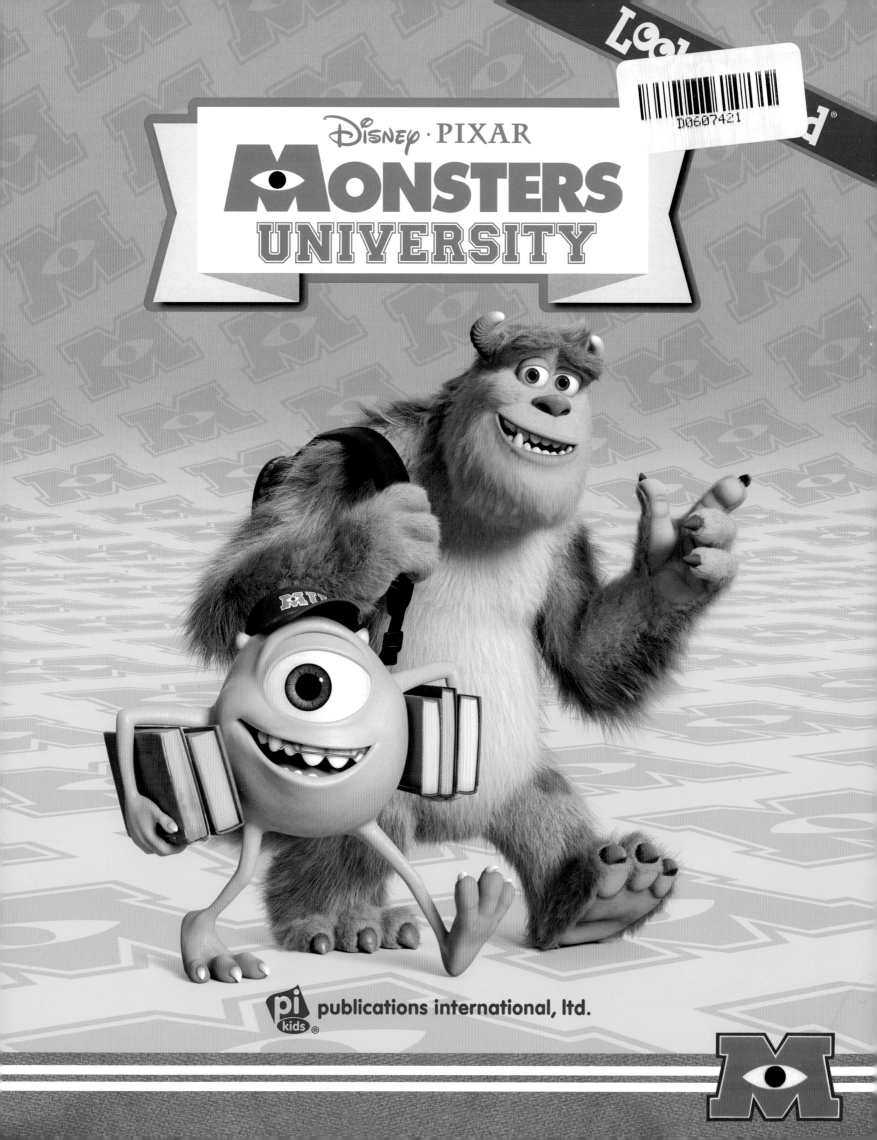

DISNEY · PIXAR

MONSTERS
UNIVERSITY

pi kids®

publications international, ltd.

When Mike arrives at Monsters University, he's amazed at the variety of students. Look around campus for these unique individuals.

Chet Alexander

Britney Davis

Percy Boleslaw

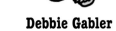

Debbie Gabler

Nancy Kim

Jay the RA

Mike and Sulley have just knocked over Dean Hardscrabble's scream can. She doesn't seem happy. Look for these school supplies in the lecture hall while Mike and Sulley try to smooth things over with the dean.

Monsters, Inc. lunch box

Glue

Calculator

Ruler

Highlighter

Monsters University backpack

Mike and Sulley have been kicked out of the Scaring Program by Dean Hardscrabble. But Mike has a plan to get back in: join a fraternity and win the Scare Games competition! Look for Mike, Sulley, and the brothers of Oozma Kappa who will take part in the big competition.

Sulley

Terri & Terry

Mike

Don

Squishy

Art

It's time for Mike and Sulley to move into the Oozma Kappa fraternity house. While they get to know their new brothers, look for these things that belong to the monsters.

Art's dream journal

Don's business card

Pair of paddles

Ms. Squibble's laundry basket

Hot cocoa

Squishy's shoes

The brothers of Oozma Kappa have to do well in this Scare Games event. The monsters need to capture their team flag while avoiding the librarian. While Mike and the rest of the Oozma Kappas go for their flag, keep an eye out for these noisy items that may draw the librarian's wrath.

Alarm clock

Bell

Radio

Bubble gum ready to pop

Bullhorn

Phone

Nails on a chalkboard

It's tight quarters in the frat house as Mike and Sulley prepare for their final Scare Games challenge! Find these special items while your two favorite monsters get ready for their next big competition.

Mike's retainer

SCARE GAMES
FINAL SIGN UP JAN. 25
PROVE YOU'RE THE BEST

Scare Games flyer

Sulley's brush & comb

Little Mikey

Mike's MU hat

SULLIVAN

Sulley's backpack

After the Scare Games, Mike sneaks into the human world to prove to everyone that he's scary. But he ends up trapped in a camp cabin with Sulley! Their only hope of getting back to the monster world is scaring so many people that they will power up the closet door. Find these frightened rangers before Mike and Sulley head back to Monsters University.

After their time at Monsters University, Mike and Sulley make it to Monsters, Inc. They're just starting off in the mail room, but great things are to come for Team Wazowski and Sullivan! Help them look for these packages and pieces of mail they have to deliver.

Fear Tech postcard

CDA stamps

Suspicious-looking package

Monster magazine

Slime magazine

Package of booger cookies

Roar Omega Roar is one of the many fraternities on campus. Go back to the college campus and look for these fraternity and sorority leaders.

Carrie Williams

Johnny Worthington

Claire Wheeler

Rosie Levin

Roy "Big Red" O' Growlahan

Carla Delgado

Sulley dreams of joining Roar Omega Roar, but it's not the only fraternity on campus. Go back to the lecture hall and look for these things owned by members of monster fraternities and sororities.

Slugma Slugma Kappa pennant

Omega Howl t-shirt

"Join Jaws Theta Chi" flyer

Python Nu Kappa jacket

Eta Hiss Hiss water bottle

Roar Omega Roar cap

Frat row is where the coolest fraternity and sorority members hang out. Head back to the Scare Games kick-off and look for these Greek letters.

Omega

Pi

Delta

Sigma

Lambda

Theta

Oozma Kappa isn't known for their fun parties or social skills. Head back to what Squishy calls "party central" and find these items that don't make for a good party.

This doily

Monster dentures

Bowl of prunes

Knitting ball and needles

Bingo card

Oozma Kappa cap

With the chaos in the library, it's going to take the librarian weeks to reorganize all the books back into the gooey decimal system! Help her find these books that need to be reshelved.

Scaring 101

Scream Can Design

Door Technology

Monstrosities

Scare Theory Vol. 7

Scream Energy

Mike and Sulley collect scare cards. Mike has six thousand...still in mint condition. Head back to their bedroom and look for a few of them.

Mike and Sulley worked hard to set up their scare in the cabin. Go back and look for these things they used to frighten the rangers.

Claw marks

Oar

Record player

Window drape

Fire poker

Fan

While getting their start at Monsters, Inc., Sulley and Mike meet some interesting coworkers. Take a look for these pictures of them!

Keep Our MAILROOM CLEAN!

Mailroom clerk

EMPLOYEE of the MONTH

Employee of the Month plaque

"Screaming" Bob Gunderson

Earl "The Terror" Thompson

"Frightening" Frank McCay

Carla KILLER CLAWS BENITEZ

Carla "Killer Claws" Benitez